re

gavotte

flying

waltz

When
Young
Melissa
SWEEPS

Finalmente! Per la mia amica e mentrice Anita Riggio.
(E, naturalmente, per Beluga.)
Colossians 3:23

—*D.S.*

Published by

PEACHTREE PUBLISHERS, LTD.

494 Armour Circle NE
Atlanta, Georgia 30324

Text © 1927, 1955, 1998 by Nancy Byrd Turner
Illustrations © 1998 by Debrah Santini

"When Young Melissa Sweeps" from MAGPIE LANE by Nancy Byrd Turner, copyright 1927 by Harcourt Brace
& Company and renewed 1995 by Nancy Byrd Turner, reprinted by permission of the publisher.

Cover and interior illustrations by Debrah Santini
Book design by Debrah Santini
Composition by Loraine M. Balcsik

Manufactured in China

10 9 8 7 6 5 4 3 2 1
First Edition

Library of Congress Cataloging-in-Publication Data

Turner, Nancy Byrd, b. 1880.
    When young Melissa sweeps / Nancy Byrd Turner; illustrated by Debrah Santini. —1st ed.
      p. cm.
    Summary: Describes how a young girl curtsies and whirls, waltzes and jigs as she sweeps the house.
    ISBN 1-56145-157-6
    [1. House cleaning—Fiction. 2. Stories in rhyme.] I. Santini, Debrah, ill. II. Title.
    PZ8.3.T851Wy 1998
    [E]—dc21   97-40941
                                                                       CIP
                                                                          AC

POEM BY
NANCY BYRD TURNER

When
Young
Melissa
SWEEPS

PAINTINGS BY
DEBRAH SANTINI

PEACHTREE
ATLANTA

When young Melissa sweeps a room
I vow she dances with the broom!

She curtsies
in a corner brightly

And leads her partner forth politely.

Then up

*and
down*

in jigs and reels,

With gold dust flying

at their heels,

They caper.

With a whirl or two

They make the wainscot shine like new;

They waltz beside the hearth, and quick

It brightens, shabby brick by brick.

A gay gavotte across the floor,

A Highland fling from door to door,

And every

crack and

corner's clean

Enough to suit a dainty queen.

If ever you are full of gloom,

Just watch Melissa

sweep a room!

curtsy

jig

Highland

caper